The Family that
LOVE BUILT

The Family that
LOVE BUILT

The Marvin and Edith Hash Family

BERNARD G. HASH

The Family That Love Built

Copyright © 2022 by Bernard G. Hash. All rights reserved.

No part of this publication may be reproduced, stored in a retrieval system or transmitted in any way by any means, electronic, mechanical, photocopy, recording or otherwise without the prior permission of the author except as provided by USA copyright law.

The opinions expressed by the author are not necessarily those of URLink Print and Media.

1603 Capitol Ave., Suite 310 Cheyenne, Wyoming USA 82001
1-888-980-6523 | admin@urlinkpublishing.com

URLink Print and Media is committed to excellence in the publishing industry.

Book design copyright © 2022 by URLink Print and Media. All rights reserved.

Published in the United States of America

Library of Congress Control Number: 2022902059
ISBN 978-1-68486-093-7 (Paperback)
ISBN 978-1-68486-094-4 (Digital)

18.01.22

Contents

Introduction 7
Chapter 1   The Beginning....................................11
Chapter 2   Our Move To Roanoke 16
Chapter 3   The Big Rescue..................................25
Chapter 4   A New Birth......................................31
Chapter 5   The Loss of A Friend.........................41
Chapter 6   The Final Son 51
Chapter 7   The Neighbors 56
Chapter 8   The Cook Out 60
Chapter 9   A Visit From A Werewolf 64
Chapter 10 The Patron List..................................69
Chapter 11 Tracy Goes to The Army...................73
Chapter 12 The Big Surprise 81
Chapter 13 Tragedy At Home 86
Chapter 14 A New Beginning 92
Chapter 15 Our First Apartment.........................98
Chapter 16 Our First CD 108

The Marvin & Edith Hash Family

Introduction

Did you ever have a story to tell but thought that no one would want to read it, or even hear it?

Well this is one of those stories. It is not about a royal family or a famous movie star. It's about a family of people who came to Virginia, The Hash Family.

Even though hundreds maybe even thousands of Hash's came this way, this is about one particular family, The Marvin and Edith Hash Family - The Untold Story.

So as you take this journey and began to reminisce with us on times past, maybe a window or a door will be opened that you can walk through to recover your own past.

Maybe, just maybe, something will be awakened in you to inspire you to begin to search for your past, and open a door for you to a whole new world. Everyone has a story to tell and this is mine. Who am I? I am Bernard G. Hash, son number 3, born Jan. 6, 1958.

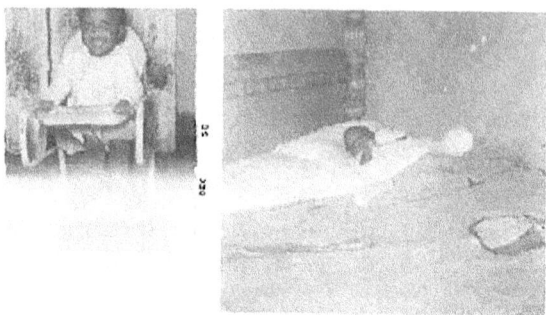

Bernard C. Hash born Jan. 6,1958

Bernard Hash 4th grade

Marvin P.L. Hash

Chapter

1

The Beginning

This is the story of a family; not a wealthy family as far as money or riches is concerned, but wealthy in many other ways. Our father and mother taught us values about life that far out weigh all the money in the world.

Father was not a king in the sense of a ruler of a country or anything like that, but he was definitely King in our house and Mom was beautiful, a Queen in her own right. She made everyone who came in our house feel like royalty.

They both taught us how to love and respect each other and how to care for one another. They told us no matter the color of your skin, you are somebody, and we could hold our heads high, because we were Hash's. And you know what? That meant something.

All of our lives, we've run into people who wanted to be like the Hash's, wanted to be around the Hash's, to look like the Hash's, and some even wanted to be Hash's.

Our family had set a standard for living a Godly life. This was something that a lot of families lacked. God put His stamp of approval on our family. And we strive each day to maintain what has been placed in us.

This story concerns the lives of ten people - a mother, a father, and eight children. We were and are a family full of love. We've all had our share of joy as well as pain.

We were and still are to this day, a family raised on Godly principles. Even though we may have strayed from time to time, we have never forgotten where we came from.

The Bible tells us to:

* "Train a child in the way he should go, and when he is old, he will not depart from it." (Proverbs 22:6)

Our parents did the best they could to teach us the way of righteousness, but each one of us must choose the path he or she must travel. My father was born in the 1930's. He was an Army man, a lean, mean, fighting machine. From the earliest time I can remember he was a Sergeant in the Army Reserve. He had already completed his active duty in The Korean War and was now an Army cook. I remember he would bring us different things home from the Army.

Two of his best friends that he would always talk about were Sgt. Hurt, and Sgt. Charles Smith. Each year they would go away to Summer Camp together. We would look forward to his return because he always brought us something special home.

We loved our father very much, but we also feared him. We knew if we had done anything wrong while he was gone, mom would tell him and we would have to face the consequences. He was very stern and believed in the Bible concerning the rod of correction.

* "Foolishness is bound in the heart of a child; but the rod of correction shall drive it far from him." (Proverbs 22:15)

My father also worked a regular job as a nurse's assistant at The Veterans Hospital in Salem Va. We would always hear him getting up to go to work. Sometimes he worked the day shift, sometimes the mid-night shift.

Mom was a very gentle woman, who loved the Lord. She would always be in the kitchen singing about the goodness of Jesus. She would sing: "When I fall on my knees with my face to the rising sun", or "Let us pray together". I can hear her just as plain as day, as if she was singing right now.

She could be classified as the Proverbs 31:10 woman, which says:" Who can find a virtuous woman? For her price is far above rubies.

*11: The heart of her husband doth safely trust in her so that he shall have no need of spoil.

*12: She will do him good and not evil all the days of her life."

As I skip on down to verse 25, this is definitely my mom.

*25: "Strength and honour are her clothing; and she shall rejoice in time to come.

*26: She openeth her mouth with wisdom; and in her tongue is the law of kindness.

*27: She looketh well to the ways of her household, and eateth not the bread of idleness.

*28: Her children rise up, and call her blessed; her husband also, and he praiseth her.

*29: Many daughters have done virtuously, but thou excellest them all.

*30: Favour is deceitful, and beauty is vain: but a woman that feareth the Lord, she shall be praised.

*31: Give her of the fruit of her hands; and let her own works praise her in the gates."

As I said, this was and is our mother. Even now she far exceeds all our expectations. No matter what she was doing, she would always be singing. We had a washing machine but no dryer, so she would hang the clothes on the clotheslines my father had placed outside. I don't know how she managed to do everything, everyday, but she always had joy.

From sun up to sun down my mom would be busy doing something; cooking, washing clothes, ironing clothes, mopping floors, folding clothes, making sure we had everything we needed.

Chapter

2

Our Move To Roanoke

I was born January 6, 1958 in a little town called Fries Va., otherwise known as Grayson Co. VA.

I really don't remember much of my early years, as I was very small and at that time the baby of the family. But I did have two brothers, Perry who was known as Doug or Number One as our other soon to be born brother called him. And Tracy was also known as Eyeball or Number Two. I became to be known as Sneaky Pete, Dirty Bert and Big Mix. I was also sometimes called Gabriel due to my trumpet playing, or Number Three. We moved from Fries when I was very young, and came to Roanoke, VA. Old Southwest, Rorer Ave.

I don't recall us having much money but I do remember every Christmas our father would always give us the greatest toys. It never mattered to us whether they were new or used we just enjoyed playing together. There would be gifts for everyone and always a bag of candy with fruit, and all kinds of nuts. They would be lined around the tree with all our names on them. The Tree would always be so beautiful with big beautiful lights, lots of ice sickles, and garland.

Pvt. Marvin P.L. Hash
Germany

We also had great uncles and aunts who always gave us gifts. Uncle Clyde and Aunt Edna only had one child at the time, so they always had something for us on Christmas Day. Also Uncle George and

Aunt Helen would buy us gifts. And then there was Uncle Earnest and Aunt Dorothy; they would send us these big boxes all the way from California.

Every Christmas Eve we would be waiting for the UPS truck to arrive because we knew something good was coming from them.

Perry Douglas Hash

Momma would be in the kitchen getting ready for the big day. Baking rolls, cakes, and sweet potato pies. She had developed a secret recipe for punch and every year she would make this big pot of punch that became known as "The Recipe". Man, you could smell the rolls baking and your mouth would begin to water, you couldn't wait for the first batch to get done.

The smell of hams and turkeys filled the air with such wonderful aromas. Mom would be in the kitchen hard at work singing Christmas Carols, going about her work, knowing that all her hard work would not be in vain. Everyone would come to our house to get a batch of Momma's rolls. And then there was her potato salad. Just thinking about it makes me hungry right now.

Having a big family has its advantages. We always had someone to talk to and someone to play with. Of course after the holidays it was back to school and back to work. Life in the Hash house was never dull or boring. When Mom was not busy she would take time out to see if we needed help with homework or anything.

We were good children, and our mother would always read many books to us, especially the Bible. Our parents believed the scriptures, like the one at Luke 6:38:

* "Give and it shall be given unto you; good measure, pressed down, shaken together, and running over, shall men give into your bosom. For with the same measure that ye mete, withal, it shall be measured back to you again."

We also read fairytales like, The Three Peas In A Pod, Puss-N-Boots, and The Emperors New Clothes, just to name a few. I developed a great love for reading and wanted to become an actor. She would always tell us we could be anything we wanted to be.

By the time I was five years old I can remember moving to Hanover Ave. N.W. to a house soon to be known as "The Honey Comb Hide Out". This house was the largest house I had ever seen. It was white and it was the biggest house on the block. You could see it from my first school, Lincoln Terrace Elementary School, which was close to a mile away.

The area became known as 'The Dump'. It was a big field that we had to cross to get to our house from school if we didn't want to walk on the sidewalk, which was the long way home. The only time we would take the long way home was when we had money to spend at Mrs. Neighbors Store.

She had a lady that worked with her named Mrs. Tutz. We never knew her real name. They were very nice to us. They had some of the best candy in that store. Banana Splits, Mint Juleps, and Now and Laters; it was a kids heaven.

There was also another store, which we frequently visited, Mrs. Banks Store. Her name was Dorothy Banks; she loved the Hash's. Any kind of candy we couldn't find at Mrs. Neighbors Store Mrs. Banks' store had. And her store was close to school, so we could stop by there and wouldn't be late to school.

Back in those days we didn't have CD players and all the electronic things that kids have today. We only had radios and eight track players. So in order to hear any music we had to listen to the one radio in the house. Everything was built into one console - the album player, the eight-track player, and the radio.

I remember sneaking and listening to music on the radio and hearing The Beatles for the first time on WROV Radio Station. I had never heard anything like that before. I heard them sing "I Want To Hold Your Hand". In our house we only listened to Gospel music. So it was a treat to hear something different for the first time. I was totally fascinated at the sound of these British guys singing.

The 60's were a great time to be alive. We had one television and it was black and white. My dad loved the westerns, so that is what we watched a lot of the time. There was Gun Smoke, The Virginian, The Big Valley, The High Chaparral, The Lone Ranger and Tonto, Zorro, Roy Rogers and Dale Evans and many, many more. However, my mom loved the Soap Operas on Channel 7, so we became very familiar with all of those characters as well. Everyday would start out with "The Price Is Right", then "The Young and The Restless", "Like sands through the hourglass so are The Days Of Our Lives", "As The World Turns", and "The Guiding Light".

Man, we thought that these were real stories about real lives, because we would always hear my Mom and my Aunt's talking about these people like they were real. They would never miss "The Stories", as they became known.

Each day we would run home from school to see "The Early Show". Back then we had an Early Show and a Late Show on T.V. They had shows like "The Little Rascals", "Tarzan", "Dark Shadows", and many more.

We also looked forward to watching The Ed Sullivan Show. This show was the highlight of our evenings. We saw groups like The Temptations, The Supremes, The Beatles, and The Jackson 5. Seeing and hearing groups like them made us want to sing even more.

By the age of six (6) I was singing in a gospel group called The Little Violinaires. The original Violinaires were our idols. We sounded just like them.

I was barely able to read or reach the microphone, but I was a singer and could learn songs very easily. My love for music grew as we traveled and had the opportunity to sing with many of the greats, like The Violinaires, The Gospel Keynotes, The Mighty Clouds OF Joy, Shirley Caesar and The Blind Boys, The Ever - Ready's and many more.

I can remember hearing James Brown for the first time - James Brown and The Famous Flames, with Maceo on the horns. I was so excited to hear the songs he would sing, like "Say It Loud, I'm Black and I'm Proud", "Papa Got A Brand New Bag", and watch him do the split and slide across the stage. The times were so much simpler back then, and music was so exciting.

I remember we would always gather in the backyard of my next-door neighbor, Joseph Hicks Jr. We would get sticks, a big one for a guitar and two little ones and some cans for drums and we would sing "I Feel Good" by James Brown.

We had the greatest times together. By this time my first sister was born. She was named Tammy Suzanne Hash. We were so much alike growing up that people thought we were twins. She was beautiful, like sunshine with two dimples. It was so nice to have a little sister. Finally someone was smaller than I was.

My older brother Tracy liked to beat on me and fight with me all the time. By age six (6), I had planned on running away several times. I would pack my clothes and go hide behind the hedge bushes until someone found me. I was small and so sad because I didn't like to be picked on because of my size.

I remember doing a lot of crazy things like eating rat poison, and taking Camphorated Oil, which could have killed me. My Mom gave me buttermilk to get me to bring it back up. I was so scared and sick. Just the smell of the buttermilk made me bring it all back up. But eventually I began to feel better.

Chapter

3

The Big Rescue

One year my brother Tracy and I were coming home from school after it had snowed all day. We were doing as kids will do. Instead of taking the long way home, we went stomping in the snow across the dump. We thought it was so exciting, stomping along, making our footprints in the snow. We were having so much fun.

All of a sudden what was so exciting was not fun anymore. Before we knew what was going on, we begin to sink into the ground. Suddenly our laughter turned to screams. Louder and louder we screamed, but no one was around to hear us.

We were already halfway in the ground when one of our neighbors, Virginia Brown, heard us screaming. She looked out her window and saw us. She began screaming for help, and she ran across the dump as fast as she could. I don't think she even took time to grab a coat.

Two other friends of ours, Larry Ashby and Charles Wright, also heard the screams and came running. They pulled us from the quicksand as fast as they could. We were covered with mud and dirt. We were crying and cold. We thanked our neighbors and also thanked God that they heard us screaming, because had they not heard us, we might still be missing today.

George & Helen Hash Family

I will never forget this experience. Even though it's been over forty years ago, it's still fresh in my mind. As I think about all the kids that go missing every year, I wonder if some of them could have met a similar fate to the one that almost took us. Our faces would have been on milk cartons and everyone would have been searching for us. How would our family have gone on without us?

That year the city came and filled in that spot with a lot of dirt. From that time on, I felt a greater love for my brother Tracy. Oh we still had our disagreements and fights, but we had a closer bond.

My first grade teacher's name was Mrs. Kearns. In second grade I had Mrs. Carey and Mrs. Bright. By the time I was in the third grade, I had my first chance to be in a play. My teacher Mrs. Travis, who later remarried and became Mrs. Franklin, took our class to try out for The Three Little Pigs. After tryouts, I was chosen for the part of the big bad wolf. I was so excited to finally have my chance to act.

My mother and father were so proud that I won the part. But as things would go, my father was away with the Army Reserve on the day that I needed to go qualify, and I was unable to find a ride.

Even though I was unable to go to the final tryouts, I never gave up on my dreams. So whenever the opportunity arose, whether in school or in church, I was always ready to learn my part and do the best job I could do.

We had a lot of different plays to do in church, *The Five Wise and Five Foolish Virgins,* The Christmas Plays, and then there were always the speeches to learn. We would spend countless hours at church and at home trying to learn our parts.

Christmas time was so exciting at our church, because we had a lot of people who really cared about the youth. They would buy us gifts each year, give us big bags of candy, and everybody loved each other so much. You could really feel the love at our church.

I remember my cousin Jeff doing a speech about "All I Want For Christmas". He had lost his front teeth and this was the perfect speech for him. He began to say his speech and everybody bust out laughing because he looked so funny. He said, "A little mouse wrote to Santa Clause and this is what he said, 'I do not wish for cheese and bread, or even something sweet. All I want for Christmas is my two front teeth' ".

Every so often I would get the opportunity to spend the night at his house. They also had a big family. There were ten of them: Tommy, Selma, Charles, John and Greg, Jane and Joyce, Jeff and Clairessa, and Stewart. These were my Uncle George and Aunt Helen's children, my daddy's brother.

Many times we would go the country, to Fries VA. where I was born, and stay with my Grand Mother Lula Johnson, and Grand Pa Hurd Johnson. There were so many of us that there were not enough bedrooms for everybody. We had to sleep in the loft or attic.

Another interesting fact is that the restroom was outside. So if anyone had to go to the restroom at night they would either have to use a can or go outside to the Johnny House. Since that was very scary because at night-time there were all these different sounds coming from the woods - the owls would be hooting and there was always the chance of a bear being out there in the woods, everyone always used the can. So every morning there would be this strong smell in the loft.

Our Great Grand Father

When morning came you would always hear our Grand Mother along with our parents in the kitchen. Ah man, you could smell the sausage, eggs, and biscuits baking. It made us so hungry. You could hear my Grand Mother singing along with my Mother. Granny Johnson would always have a bag of horehound candy and some Doctor Peppers. That was her favorite soda pop. Soda pop was only a nickel back then. And you could also save the bottles and sell them each for a penny. We had the greatest times.

When I was about six years old, I remember my Grand Pa dying. They said he was in church giving his testimony and he had a heart attack. It was the saddest day that I could recall in my life up until that time. What a terrible way to die I thought. But then I realized, this is what he believed in, so if you have to go, why not go doing what you like. And my Grand Pa was doing what he liked. He was in church when he went to be with the Lord. My Granny Johnson was alone now, and she did not want to leave her home. She stayed in Fries, VA for along time, until her health began to give out on her. Then she came to Roanoke to live with My Uncle George and Aunt Helen.

My Aunt May also lived in Fries and she watched out for her as much as she could. She had a dog-named Sampson, a white German shepherd. She loved that dog and brought him to Roanoke as well.

Chapter

A New Birth

By this time child number five (5) was born. She was named Valerie Germane Hash. She really had a set of lungs on her and a beautiful smile. She was so funny.

We were also blessed to have some of the best cousins. My Uncle Clyde and Aunt Edna, who were like second parents to us, had a daughter named Deidra Darlene Hash and they came from Baltimore, Maryland to live with us.

My father and two of his brothers, Uncle Clyde and Uncle George, fought in The Korean War together. And the funny part is, these three brothers married three sisters.

Marvin, who is my father, married Edith. My uncle Clyde married Edna, and George married Helen. And thus it began, the replenishing of the earth. *Gen: 9:1 says: "And God blessed Noah, and his sons, and said unto them, be fruitful and multiply, and replenish the earth." Hash's began to spring up every year.

There was always a lot of excitement in our house, because Uncle Clyde was so funny. His feet were frost bitten in the war and they wanted to amputate them. I remember it was hard to stay in the same room with him because of the smell of his feet, but he always made you feel so good, and made you laugh so much, that you never wanted to leave him.

Uncle Clyde had a job working for an ice cream company named Hershey's Ice Cream. He drove the truck and he would always bring us these big brown containers of ice cream. We were in heaven.

Before it was time to get his feet cut off, my Uncle accepted The Lord and he was healed. This was my first recollection of a miracle. I saw my uncle's feet and they were rotten, and then all of a sudden they were not anymore. The doctor's could not believe what had happened. It reminds me of what Luke 9:11 says; "And the people when they knew it, followed him; and he received them, and spake unto them of the kingdom of God, and he healed them that had need of healing".

My Uncle Clyde and Aunt Edna would always come, pick me up, and take me places. I remember them coming to get me early one morning. They took me to Fries Va. to see my Aunt May. They bought me sodas and honey buns. When I was younger I would get carsick, so I didn't like to ride in cars too much, especially around curves. And there were a lot of curves to get to Fries. Once I got there though I was fine.

I met my cousin Cathy, and this boy named Buster. Cathy lived with my Aunt May who was my mom's, my Aunt Edna, and Aunt Helen's sister. Aunt May's husbands name was Uncle Warren. He was a big man and had a deep voice. He was very nice. Every time I see my cousin Jeanny, she reminds me of him.

One day I heard two girls singing at a church there called Taylor's Chapel. Their names were Linda and Cora Young. They could really sing and they sang a song called "Just The Two Of Us". I will never forget that song because they sang it so well.

My Uncle George use to preach there a lot, and our group sang there often as well. Everyone loved our group. We had voices like angels and our moves were like the original Fantastic Violin-Aires.

Around this time my Aunt Ann passed away. She was also one of my mother's sisters. She was married to Uncle Walt Green. They lived in Austinville, Virginia. I didn't know Aunt Ann very well because I was so young when she passed.

Aunt Ann and Uncle Walt had several children; Ramona, Patricia who we just called Trish, and then there was Carl. The day she passed was another sad day. First my Grand Pa, and now my Aunt Ann. My Uncle Walt was never the same after that day.

Ramona could really sing too. We called her "Shoes" because she loved shoes so much. She use to sing a song called, "Here We Go Sweeping Through The City". She would tear that song up, and have the whole church shouting and praising God.

She is the one who gave me the nick name of Sneaky Pete, because she caught me in the cookie jar one day stealing cookies when my mom had told me I couldn't have any more. But they were so good I couldn't help myself. Ramona was the one who found me hiding under the table eating cookies.

My Mom also had one brother, Uncle Mitchell Johnson. He married my Aunt Ruby. They also had several children; Jerry, Gordon, Steve known as Ted, Charlotte, and Sharon.

A few years later they divorced and Uncle Mitchell then married my Aunt Gladys. My Uncle Mitch was the only man I knew that could drive up Bent Mountain with a whole onion in one hand, be passing two and three cars at a time going around curves, taking big bites out of the onion, and never have a wreck. We would be down in the floor with tears in our eyes from the onion and scared to death. Aunt Gladys, who I called Gladys Knight, always got a kick out of that. She would be sitting beside him and not even be crying.

One year we had to go sing in Independence Va. My Uncle Mitch was there. When we began to sing a song called "Jesus You've Been Good To Me" my Uncle Mitch went off. He started clapping his hands like a wild man, knocking over chairs, and praising God.

Cpl. George Bush

We were trying to sing and keep a straight face, but trying to hold in the laughter it was killing us inside. We were just kids and we had never seen anyone act like that before at any of our concerts. We were no more good. Alvin and Steve were trying their best not to laugh, but that night we couldn't help it.

We also had a cousin named Whitfield Carter. He was the slowest driver in the world. If the speed limit was 25, he would do 15. He made sure that he never got a ticket for speeding. He use to take us to North Wilkesboro N.C. and it seemed like we would never get there sometimes because he would drive so slow.

But he was a very nice man, and a good cousin. He owned a truck and he really knew how to use it to make money. He would take us around to different stores and we would get loads of cardboard, metal, and different things that you could make money off of. He always had money, and he would share it with us sometimes, but he wouldn't give us much. He had two sons; one named Larry who we called Peter, and then there was Buzz. He also had one daughter named Evie.

We had Conventions back then, Missionary Conventions, and Sunday School Conventions. Everyone would be so excited as they got ready to go. People would come from all over the U.S. Everyone was so kind and fellowship was so great.

Then there was The General Assembly. Everyone came to that. People would let you stay in their houses and they would cook at the churches so everyone would have something to eat.

Ramona Martin

And then it happened. Like everything else as they always say: "All good things must come to an end", and it did. People stopped letting people stay in their homes, and every one had to come up with extra money for hotels. If you had a big family it became too expensive.

Back in those days we also had Youth Camps. Our cousin Leonard Hash, who was called "The Brain", orchestrated them. One year at a youth camp in Princeton W. Virginia, there was this organ player named Kevin who was from Winston Salem, N.C. Every time he would play, the spirit got high, and he would have a fainting spell. When he passed out the music would stop and there was no one else to play the organ. So my Uncle Clyde said, "I got a remedy for that. The next time he passes out, I'll fix him."

Sure enough, Kevin passed out the next night. Uncle Clyde and some more of us picked him up and carried him to the back room. My Uncle Clyde broke open a pack of smelling salt (Ether) and shoved it up his nose, and when he came to, he never passed out again. It was so hilarious. We all cried laughing. My brother Darryl got saved and filled with The Holy Ghost at one of these camp meetings.

Chapter

5

The Loss of A Friend

Now it was time to have a name for our group. So after many hours and days of trying to come up with a name, my mother said we should be named The Royal-Aires, because we represented royalty and we had royal blue suits. We liked the name and decided to add Fantastic to it. So we became The Fantastic Royal-Aires.

Our group was going along well; we had cut our first record, titled " I Want To Be Ready", with "When The Roll Is Called Up Yonder" on side two. Our Manager, Mr. James Green, was doing a great job for us. A few years later he was killed by accident, and Uncle Clyde became our manager, with my father as assistant manager.

Our Group consisted of several members: Perry Hash was the bass player and high tenor, Tracy was the lead singer, and Alvin Reynolds was the lead guitar player who could play anything. He taught us how to harmonize because he had been a member of another group before he came to us. Steve Hayes was one of our back up singers. He later became lead guitar player. John Hash was another back up singer, Greg Hash was back up and lead singer, Jeff Hash, who didn't do much singing, became known as The Professional Hand Clapper. And last but not least was myself, Bernard Hash, back up and lead singer.

We had several other members along the way, but these were the originals. Later came Paul Craig, Eugene Hash, Vernon Williams, and Valdez Gill who was the best drummer I had ever seen. Still later my brother Phillip sang with us, and Derrail Reynolds became our drummer.

We began traveling to different states, singing the gospel. One year we even sang in Washington

D.C., right up the street from The White House. That morning we were on the radio singing and that evening we were singing in a Town Hall, up the street from The Capital.

I remember on the way home we stopped at a Pancake House for breakfast and had some of the best pancakes I had ever tasted. They thought we were The Jackson 5, and treated us like royalty that day. Wow, what a wonderful time we had.

By this time child number 6 was born to our family. Her name is Gloria Michele Hash. Later my sisters decided to form a group along with some cousins, Deidra, and Jane, along with two close friends from church, Angela Gills and Pamela Fuel.

They became the Royal-Lets, and we began to travel together with Uncle Clyde and my Dad. During this time we were part of a body of churches called The C. O.G. A. - The Church Of God Apostolic. We had Jubilee's every first Saturday of each month.

We would travel from Roanoke to N. Carolina (St. Peters Church) to Wytheville Va. (Morning Star Church) to Chatham Va. (St. Paul Church) to Galax, to Pulaski, Woodlawn, and Independence Va. Every church would host the Jubilee. We would come together; each choir and groups from all over to be a part of this great function.

We had such a wonderful time at the Jubilee's. Uncle Paul would sing "Got On My Traveling Shoes". It was a time of fellowship and we got to spend time with the youths from other churches. We looked forward to the Jubilee each month. We didn't care how far away it was or how late we stayed, we wanted to be there, and our Uncle Clyde always got us there. We would travel in rain, snow or sleet to be with all the other youth. We made so many friends; it was some of the best years of our lives.

However, during the late 70's early 80's the Jubilee's began to change. Gas prices started to rise, our Uncles were getting older, and no one wanted to travel anymore. The format also began to change. Instead of all singing, they decided that we were not getting enough of the word. So they started to just have singing for about an hour and a half and then have a sermon.

The Jubilee's went downhill from there. People stopped traveling the distance because it was too much trouble to go all that way to sing two songs, and then sometimes you didn't even get to sing.

By this time child number 7 was born. His name is Darryl Spencer Hash. Our family was growing so fast. My dad was working very hard to take care of all of us. It seemed like no matter how many children there were, we always had plenty. My mom could take anything in the kitchen (food wise) and make a meal out of it.

We may have had a lot of brown beans and corn bread, but we never went hungry. Our mom could cook better than anyone. She could bake pies, cakes, and cookies from scratch. Momma would bake Flako Corn Bread and put butter between each slice. That made it taste so good.

When she was in the kitchen she would start singing and praising God, and it seemed like God always multiplied everything we had. Birthdays were special for each child because she made them all special. We were blessed, as Deuteronomy 28:1-14 says:

*1:And it shall come to pass, if thou shalt hearken diligently unto the voice of the Lord thy God, to observe and to do all his commandments which I command thee this day, that the Lord thy God will set thee on high above all nations of the earth.

*2: And all these blessings shall come on thee, and overtake thee, if thou shalt hearken unto the voice of the Lord thy God.

*3. Blessed shalt thou be in the city (and we were) blessed shalt thou be in the field.

*4: Blessed shall be the fruit of thy body, and the fruit of thy ground, and the fruit of thy cattle, the increase of thy kine, and the flocks of thy sheep.

Uncle Paul's Family

*5: Blessed shall be thy basket and thy store.

*6: Blessed shalt thou be when thou comest in, and blessed shalt thou be when thou goest out.

*7: The Lord shall cause thine enemies that rise up against thee to be smitten before thy face: they shall come out against thee one way, and shall flee before thee seven ways.

*8: The Lord shall command the blessing upon the in thy storehouse (and He did) and in all that thou settest thine hand unto; and he shall bless thee in the land which the Lord thy God giveth thee.

*9: The Lord shall establish thee an holy people unto himself, as he hath sworn unto thee, if thou shalt keep the commandments of the Lord thy God, and walk in his ways.

*10: And all the people of the earth shall see that thou art called by the name of the Lord; and they shall be afraid of thee.

*11: And the Lord shall make thee plenteous in goods, in the fruit of thy body (and He did) and in the fruit of thy cattle, and in the fruit of thy ground, in the land which the Lord sware unto thy fathers to give thee.

*12: The Lord shall open unto thee his good treasure, the heaven to give the rain unto thy land in his season, and to bless all the work of thine hand: and thou shalt lend unto many nations, and thou shalt not borrow.

*13. And the Lord shall make thee the head, and not the tail; and thou shalt not be beneath; if thou hearken unto the commandments of the Lord thy God, which I command thee this day, to observe and to do them:

*14: And thou shalt not go aside from any of the words which I command thee this day, to the right hand, or to the left, to go after other gods to serve them.

Gods has truly kept his word and established this family in the Roanoke Valley, The State of Virginia, the Nation, and the World.

The Fantastic Revelaires — Gospel Singing Group

Chapter

6

The Final Son

So, once again, there was another child born, - Number Eight. He was named Phillip Andrew Hash. Phillip was special in his own way. I had to teach him everything because he looked up to me. I had to bathe him, and whenever he had to go to the bathroom, he would call me. No matter what I was doing, I could be in the street playing football with the guys or anywhere else, but I could always hear his call. He would say " Na Na Boo Boo", and I would have to stop what I was doing so I could go take care of baby brother.

Everybody always laughed, because it was so funny, to hear him say, NA NA BOO BOO. It was like he would be screaming it so loud that everybody in the neighborhood could hear him.

Now our Family was complete. There were five (5) boys and three (3) girls. My oldest brother, Doug was so cool, because he got to do everything first. I remember his first girlfriend. Her name was Jean.

And even though he had lots of girlfriends, Jean was the first I remember in Roanoke.

Another I remember is Cindy Carter, who had a sister named Renea. They went to Garden of Prayer No. 7, Pastor, Shadrack Browns church. But Doug was very serious about Jean. I remember him being so in love with her that he challenged daddy to go see his girlfriend. He wanted to see her so bad, and my dad told him he couldn't go. They began to argue and then fight. My brother ran out the house and headed for the dump.

My dad stopped, picked up a two by four, and started chasing him across the dump. I was so afraid for him, because I thought daddy was going to kill him. But Tracy and I knew if he could get away with this it would open up the door for us.

And then it happened, Tracy fell in love with Cookie, whom some of you may know her as Karen Walker or Karen C. She is a very popular radio personality now at W. T. O. Y. in Roanoke, Va. When this happened, Tracy began to sneak out the house.

My first girlfriends name was Priscilla Holmes. She lived in Pulaski, Va., which was so far away, all we could do was write each other. But it seemed like girls were always attracted to me because I was a singer.

Even though I really cared about Priscilla, it was very hard for me to remain faithful to her. We were traveling all the time, and so many girls were falling in love with me. It was very hard trying to talk to all of them, especially when several of them would be at church at the same time.

I'm not giving their names to be boastful or anything, but they were all very special to me. There was Pamela Fuel, Carmen Davis, and Darlene Grubb, who use to write me some of the most beautiful letters.

from top to bottom- Virginia Brown, Peggy Barnes, Tammy Hash, Deidra Dews & Gloria Hash

Then, in 1970, when our schools became mixed, I was sitting behind the most beautiful girl in the world, or so I thought at the time. Her name was Doris Damron. She never knew I liked her though.

Next was Janie Ingram. One year we went to perform at a banquet in Wytheville Va., and there was the most beautiful young lady I had ever seen. She was from Winston Salem, N. Carolina. My brother Doug also liked her as well, but I won her in the end. For the first time in my life, I knew I was in love. I wanted to be around her all the time. But then again the distance thing got in the way. I lived in Roanoke and she lived in N. Carolina, so our relationship didn't last very long.

And through them all was Priscilla, still in love with me. But by now I was too far-gone. I didn't know who I wanted to be with anymore. There were also the girls at my church, Lisa Johnson, Cheryl Burnet and the girls at school, Ellen Burch and Tonya Baker.

Eventually I went to a church to hear the Gospel Keynotes sing and I was introduced to Kathy Casey. And so it began again. We were still traveling and singing, and I would always meet somebody else. Kathy was sort of out of my league, but she was fun to be around. I remember walking for miles, down to Tinker Creek Apts. to see her.

I thought, at last I had finally found the right girl for me. We spent countless hours on the phone. It didn't matter if we ever said anything or not, just knowing the other person was on the phone was all that mattered.

She had a brother named Leonard Casey, and he became my best friend. We went everywhere together. We would go to Washington Park and play basketball and horseshoes. We always looked out for each other.

Proverbs 18:24 says,

* 24: A man that has friends must shew himself friendly: and there is a friend that sticketh closer than a brother.

We definitely made a lot of friends. Friends we still have even to this day.

Chapter

7

The Neighbors

It seems like everyone in the neighborhood would come to our house to play. We played from sun up to sun down; Kick ball, Hop Scotch, One Two Three Red Light, Mother May I, Cowboys and Indians, we would shoot Marbles, and play Hide And Seek. Only we would say, "hide in a bee bow, jack o see bow, time I count to ten, you better be ready, 1, 2, 3, 4, 5, 6, 7, 8, 9, 10". And while the person who was "it" was counting, everyone would run and try to find the best hiding place. You had to try to find each person and beat him or her back to home base.

There was always something to do on our street. We had the best neighbors. Next door to us were the Browns. There was the father Floyd Brown, the mother Hilda Brown, June, Robert who we called Jerome, Floyd Jr. who we just called Pee Wee, William known as Stinker, Thomas known as Bo Bo, and then there was Virginia who was called Sissy.

We were all very close, although we had a competition going on with them all the time. They wanted to be better than us. We had our Gospel group, and they had their R&B band. So as we practiced, it was as if we would see who could get the loudest.

It was so funny, when I think back on all of it, because as all children do, we would make fun of each other. As I said before, my dad did not spare the rod and since they were next door to us, they could hear every time we got a beating. So when we would come outside to play, they would be snickering and picking fun at us.

But they had problems with their speech, which we would laugh about. For instance, they would call their mother "Yella". Now the woman's name was Hilda, so where did they get "Yella" from? They would say, "Yella can I have some cearls," instead of cereal. And, "Yella, can we go play in the screet". They could never say street. Then they would ask for a "lonny sandwich" because they could not say Bologna sandwich.

Everyday we would laugh so hard at them we would be crying. We are still good friends to this date. When we see each other, we holler at each other. Sissy will holler, "Uncle Marvin", and I'll holler back, "YELLA".

Across the street from us was the Sayles family: Mrs. Cherry, Deborah, Wayne and Kevin. Later on Mr. Moe moved in their house after they moved out.

Next to them was Mrs. Florence. And then there was Mrs. Katie, Cathy, and Cheryl Evans. Next to them were Mr. and Mrs. Roy Barnes. They had a son named Timothy and a daughter named Peggy.

On down a little further was The Hairston family: Mrs. Hairston, Linda, Faye, Joe, Thomas and Ronnie. Across the street from them were Johnny Smoke and his family: Anthony, Lisa, Sofia, Mary Ann, and a few others.

Coming back up the street was Mr. Franklin, who had pear and cherry trees in his yard. We were always climbing his trees to get some pears because they were so good. And his cherries were so big and sweet. He had some friends that would always come over his house, named Rama and Nelson.

Next door to him were The Browns as I mentioned, and then us. On our other side were the Dobson / Hick's family. Mrs. Alice Dodson was a famous nightclub singer. And Mr. Dodson was so cool. He always wore these fine hats. Even when I see him now he always has on a fine hat. Their son was named Joseph Hicks Jr., who became my best friend in those days.

Next to them was the Gaither/Cotton family. There was Mr. and Mrs. Cotton, Laverne, Linda, Anita, Charlotte, and Ness. Then there was David Hamm who we always called The Good Shepherd. Next to him was Mr. Lewis who came to be known as Speedy, because he always walked so fast.

Across the street from him was Mrs. Whitt, who lived in a pink house. She had two young grand daughters who lived with her, named Gail and Ann Thomas. Up from them were Mrs. Carol and Mr. Dickey. We had a cousin named Mildred who stayed with them.

Chapter

8

The Cook Out

During the 70's our neighbors threw some of the best cookouts. Mrs. Florence and Mrs. Carol would always invite us to the cookouts. They would grill and play music by The Four Tops, like "Sugar Pie Honey Bun" and The Temptations, singing " My Girl". We ate some of the best hamburgers and hot dogs.

We also met so many different people who came over from the Lincoln Terrace Projects. There was Dana, Tony, and Charlie Fraction, Larry Ashby, Charles Wright, Mr. and Mrs. Bumbry, and their daughter Toy, and the Walker family; Gail, Randy, Lee Lee, and Janice. Other Lincoln Terrace visitors were a girl named Laverne who works for the City of Roanoke now, Todd, Vestell, and Keith who we called Mr. Moony, and Vestell's sister named Hellena who was such a funny person. Our street was busy, and Central Station was The Honey Comb Hideout, our home.

Every now and then we would go down to Addison to play football in the big field, and these two brothers would be down there named, Sammy and David Johnson. We called David Mr. Buggers, because his nose would always be running and he would wipe the buggers on his clothes.

There were a lot of elderly people in our neighborhood who couldn't get to the store for themselves, so they would ask us to go for them. Of course in those days, the 70's, everything at the store was a lot less. Sometimes they would tell us to keep the change, maybe fifty cents, maybe less. But fifty cents in those days was like being rich. You could go to the store and get 100 pieces of candy or cookies two for a penny.

There was a family who lived across the dump in a green house that we always went to the store for, even though the store was only a little way from them. The son's name was Michael. He would call me Mr. Store. His mother was so nice also. They could have gone to the store for themselves, but they enjoyed having us race across the dump to get to their house. It was very nice just to see them too.

My sister Tammy and I would race to see who could get to their house first to go to the store for them. One day I told my sister not to ride my bike because I had some problems with the chain popping on me. But do we ever listen? My sister Tammy got on my bike and took off. She was determined that she was going to go to the store for Mrs. Hairston that day. So just as I had warned her, the chain popped and sent Tammy flying through the air.

The next thing I knew here comes Tammy, crying and holding her mouth, because the bike had knocked two of her front teeth out. After we knew she was all right, we all cried laughing at her because she looked so funny without her two front teeth. I can remember that day just like it was yesterday. It seemed like there was always so much excitement in our house.

One time I was running through the back yard and there was this plank laying in the yard. I didn't see the nail sticking up and as soon as I ran across it, a rusty nail went right through my right foot. I screamed, pulled my foot up off the plank, and ran in the house to my father. My foot got very infected. Daddy was a nurse's assistant at the Veterans Hospital and we didn't have a lot of money, so daddy was our doctor most of the time. He knew a lot about cleaning wounds.

He squeezed my foot so hard, I was boo - hooing and crying, I was in so much pain. Then, he wrapped my foot with gauze pads and kept the sore area clean and bandaged. He was a good doctor. If he thought we needed to go to the doctor though, he would always take us to Burrell Memorial Hospital.

One year my sister Valerie was getting ready to take a bath. As she began to run her water she turned on the hot water. For some reason that day the water was hotter than usual. So as Valerie stepped into the water she screamed. The next thing we knew she came running through the house screaming and crying. All the skin had come off her feet. It was very scary to see her feet with no skin on them. Again, daddy came to the rescue. We were fortunate to have someone with medical skills in our family.

Valerie was not a big girl, in fact she was very skinny. As Madea might say, she was "skinty". We called her Ms. Bones as her knick name. In fact, we all had knick names. My sister Gloria became Ms. Goof because she was so crazy and would always do stupid stuff to try and make us laugh. Tammy's nickname was Suzzie Q. or Tammy Sue. And Phillip's nickname was Baby Ma-bow or Pooch.

Chapter

9

A Visit From A Werewolf

Speaking of knick names, this story is funny. My brother Darryl became known as the werewolf. It so happens we were all sitting in our room around 10:00 o'clock one night watching The Night Of The Were Wolf. Doug and Tracy were there as well as Johnny Smoke and myself. We told Darryl to go to bed, but he refused. He wanted to be a big boy and stay up. He was about nine or maybe ten years old at the time. So we let him watch.

About halfway through the movie, all of a sudden he rises up just like a Vampire and begins howling like a werewolf. We thought he was just playing at first, so we told him to shut up and sit down.

But this was serious; he began to howl louder and louder. My daddy hollowed up the steps and told us to be quite. We were about to get in trouble now. So we began to slap Darryl but none of that worked. He began to get louder and louder. By this time my daddy was mad and on his way up the stairs with the switches. So we grabbed Darryl and began to take him downstairs to daddy.

Johnny Smoke didn't make things any better because he was laughing so hard that he had all of us laughing till we were crying. Daddy began to holler at Darryl to get him to shut up the noise, but that didn't work.

Darryl just began to howl even more. Finally my Dad took him to the emergency room at Community Hospital. Darryl howled all the way to the hospital.

The doctor put a brown paper bag over his head, and then he stopped. The doctor said he was hyperventilating, and couldn't catch his breath. He said it was a good thing that we brought him to the hospital when we did. We laughed and laughed for days. Even now when I see him I think about that day, and it makes me laugh. I had never seen anything happen like that before.

Everybody used to come to our house, and we use to have a lot of fun together with the different guys from the hood. We would sit up all night telling jokes and ranking on each other. We would wait to see who would fall asleep first. Then, we would take off their shoes and put matches between their toes. One time we got my oldest brother Doug good. He was in bed and his feet were sticking out from under the covers. Johnny Smoke said "Bert", which was what he called me, "come here Bert, look." We got a book of matches, placed one between each of his toes, and lit them.

Doug's foot slid under the covers. It was hilarious. He was so mad at us.

But he couldn't do anything because he had gotten us before as well. We did some crazy things to each other. I'm just glad no one ever got hurt.

We would go to Pop Eye and Brownie's grocery store (Joe Monsuers) to get doughnuts, a lot of snacks, and just stay up telling jokes all night. There was Patrick and Raymond Phelps who we called Pellet, Johnny Smoke, Leonard Casey, Tracy, Doug, Pee Wee, and myself.

One year Doug and Johnny Smoke got a job working at Kenny Burger. Each night they would bring home all kinds of chicken, those little doughnut rolls, and French Fries. It was so good.

We would get so hungry waiting for them to get off from work. But it was well worth the wait when they walked through the door. You could smell that Kenny's chicken, and the rolls were so good.

Johnny Smoke was the best basketball player in the neighborhood. He always had money and would always bribe us to do things for him. We knew that if we didn't, we would not get any doughnuts or candy from him.

Johnny Smoke would always drink a quart of milk and smoke cigarettes. He loved to run track. I believe he could have been a famous track star or basketball player had he taken care of his self. But he couldn't stop smoking, which is how he got his knick name, Johnny Smoke. His real name was Jonathan Smith.

He could tell jokes that would have you crying laughing all day and night. Just the look on his face would make you laugh. So we always tried to stay on his good side.

One year Darryl got into trouble and got a beating for it. We were all sitting in the living room laughing at him, because he would always tell on us and get us in trouble. Now it was his time, and Johnny Smoke just kept on making him laugh so he would get another beating. Daddy was telling Darryl to shut up and be quite. But Johnny Smoke would make him bust out laughing again, and he would get another beating. It was finally payback time. Darryl was like the family snitch, he would always sneak and tell Daddy or Momma on us, when we did something wrong. So we were happy to see him get his beatings, because he would always get away with everything. By this time our dad was starting to mellow out due to his age and he didn't give us beatings as much anymore. So to see Darryl finally get his really made our day.

Johnny Smoke liked to hear us sing and he would always try to sing like Paul Beasley of the Gospel Keynotes. We would laugh so hard because he could not sing. He sounded like a chimpanzee. We gave him a new knick name, Lance Link, Secret Chimp. You would have to hear him and see him to really understand what I'm saying.

One year my dad brought home some Mince Meat Pies. These pies were like laxatives. We told Johnny Smoke not to eat them but he didn't listen to us. He just kept going back getting slice after slice. All of a sudden, after about 30 minutes, Johnny started knelling over. His stomach had started to hurt, and those Mince Meat pies were working on him. If only you had been there to see the look on his face. We laughed so hard. This was the first time we were not only laughing with him, but we were laughing at him. It became known as The Mince Meat Pie Incident.

Chapter

10

The Patron List

The Hash family was well known. Everyone would come to our house to buy dinners, doughnuts, and candy bars because we were always selling something to raise money for the church or for our groups.

We had a patron list and would go from door to door to ask people for donations. There were companies that had fundraiser products to help organizations raise money.

You talk about eating some candy bars and boxes of candy. We really would end up eating a lot of the product. It was hard to be in that house with all that candy in the pantry and not eat your share.

We had Polly Wog's, Chocolate Mint Melt A-Ways, and these big Chocolate bars. My Uncle Clyde would load us all in his station wagon and we would sell doughnuts or candy bars all day. We raised so much money.

This is how we met Mr. Cunningham from the projects. He loved to come and buy dinners from the

Hash's. When he saw us he would always ask us: "When will ya'll be selling another dinner?"

By this time a lady named Mrs. Cat and her two sons, Ronnie and Gary, moved in across the street. At first we didn't get along with them. But they were so funny, especially Ronnie. Johnny Smoke would always pick at him. His speech was not very good then, and he would say, "I'm gon tell my mom on lou." He could not say "you", he would always say "lou".

We had so much fun growing up. Across the dump was The Lincoln Terrace Projects, and some of the people who lived there would come to our neighborhood to start trouble. We would have rock battles and get into fights with them.

One year there was a rumor going around about The Monkey Man. This terrorized the neighborhood. It was during the 70's and we were afraid to walk to school. Even the teachers would lock all the windows and keep the doors locked all day. We would not stay in the park long; we would make sure we were at home before dark. There were also a lot of gangs starting to form back then. Things were beginning to become dangerous after dark.

We were lucky to have a park right down the street from us. We would run down the hill to get to the park to try and beat each other to the swings. There was this one water fountain at the end of the park, and there was always someone there trying to drink all the water. There was also a spring at Washington Park, where this water would come out of the mountain. It was the best tasting water.

As years went by, the Dump began to sink, and the street became slumped. The dump had to be closed for repairs. Years later they repaired the dump and added a swimming pool and new parking lots.

The Project has been upgraded now also, but all the houses on the 400 block of Hanover Ave, are still there. We lived at 401 Hanover Ave. N.W. Our house caught on fire several times and we had to move away, but we always returned.

Over the years I have had several bumps and bruises. One year we were playing in the house and somebody picked me up and threw me over the banister. I hit my head on the radiator. This was my first concussion.

Another day we were playing softball at the dump and my cousin Deidra was batting. I was the hind catcher, and when she let go of the bat it hit me in the forehead. A huge knot came up on my head. This was my second concussion. We had to go and sing that night in Galax, Virginia. After we had got through singing, a girl named Janet Blair came up and kissed me on my knot.

Then there was another incident when I was playing football in the street. I was going for the long bomb and not looking where I was going. I ran smack into the telephone poll. I was knocked out cold. This gave me my third concussion.

PFC Bernard G. Hash
United States Marines
1927

Chapter

11

Tracy Goes to The Army

Later that year my brother Tracy decided to go to the Army. This brought about big changes in our house as well as our group. He was our lead singer. How would we ever survive without him?

Several of us tried to keep the group going but things began to go downhill. We really depended on him, and it was not fun any more without him. Nobody wanted to lead, so Uncle Clyde would take the microphone and sing. His favorite songs which were, "Jesus Loves Me" and "His Eye is On The Sparrow."

About three or four months later Tracy came back home. He was born with asthma and he was unable to do the training. This asthma condition had plagued him from birth. It had taken his life as a child, but my dad and my mom along with my Aunt Edna prayed over him and he came back to life. He received a medical discharge from The Army. Soon after his return, he went on the road with another gospel group named Willie Banks, and some others. Things would never be the same.

Tracy later got married to Beverly. To this union was born three children; Maurice, Tiffany, and Tracy Jr. But as it would happen, Tracy got divorced. He later got re-married to Marilene Toliver. The Royal-Aires still tried to carry on, but to no avail. Without our star singer there would be no more Royal-Aires. Different ones tried to take up the mantle, but it never lasted long.

Each time Tracy would come back home, we would try again. But it just wasn't there anymore. Still, we always could sing together, no matter how long we had been apart. Even with no rehearsals, things just always clicked when we got together to do a concert or just around the family table.

One day as I was coming out of the old Jefferson Theatre, a Marine Corps Sergeant approached me. Johnny Smoke and I had just gone to see the new Bruce Lee movie " Enter The Dragon". The sergeant grabbed me by the arm and told me to come on in. He began to ask me questions about whether I liked money or not and if I would like to travel. To each question my answer was yes. Before I knew it, he had already talked me into going into The Marines. My Uncle Earnest, whom I was named after, was a marine. It just seemed like the right thing to do at the time. My Uncle's name was Earnest Grant Hash, and my name is Bernard Grant Hash. I wanted to be like him, so I said yes. I wanted to make him proud, but I didn't think about how much it would hurt my mom. She never thought that someone as small as me would want to go into The Marines. I was only 119 pounds and about 5ft. 6in. I really knew nothing about being a soldier except what I had picked up from my dad.

But before all this happened my sister Tammy got married to one of the members of our group, Alvin Reynolds our guitar player. They had a son named Derrail. He was the coolest little guy. My sister worked at Halmode Apparel and she loved it. While she worked I had the opportunity to help take care of her son. I had so much fun with Derrail; it was like he was mine. When I went off to The Marine Corps, I really missed him.

I went away to Basic Training at San-Diego Recruit Depot in San Diego California. I left home in April 1977 and returned home in August 1977. Those four months I was away were some of the hardest times of my life. I had never been away from home for so long.

Before I went away, I had been dating a girl named Theresa A. Jeffries for a few years and I was in love with her. It broke her heart to see me go away. We met at True-Vine Church one night when we were singing there. We began to spend a lot of time together. I would walk for miles to get to her house. She lived on Ferncliff Ave. and I lived in the 400 block of Hanover. It was a long walk but I was still too young to drive and didn't have a bike at the time. So I really didn't mind the walk.

Her mother was very nice to me, but I don't think her father liked me very much. She had a younger brother named Jeff Jr., an older brother named Ricky, and two beautiful older sisters named Dee Dee and Loretta who was nick named (Mutt). They were cool.

But as fate would have it, I was up to my old ways and I had gotten another girl pregnant although I didn't know about it. She went to our church and her name was Deborah Robinson. I asked her before I went away to the marines if the child was mine, but she denied it. She said the child was by another young man she was seeing and they were getting married.

So I never thought anymore about it. After Basic Training I returned home. Boy was it good to see everyone again. As soon as I got off the plane, my Mom and Dad, along with Theresa were waiting for me. I didn't look the same though. I left home with one of the biggest Afro's in Roanoke, and came home bald.

I felt strange, but no one seemed to care about how funny I looked, they were just glad to see me. When I got to Momma's house, Derrail ran up to me and kicked me in the shin and took off running. He had on some of those hard baby shoes, and it really hurt. I wanted to cry, but I was a Marine, and Marines don't feel pain.

I spent most of my leave time with Theresa, whom we all called Snookie. I was 19 and she was 17. The day came when it was time to leave to go to Camp Pendleton California and wait to be flown to my Duty Station in Hawaii. One night when I was on the phone with her long distance she told me that she was having my baby. So I had to go to my Commanding Officer and request military leave to go home to marry her.

My leave was approved and I was on my way home again. But before I left, I had to make arrangements with a buddy of mine, Sergeant Chester Gill, to have somewhere to stay when I came back with my wife. He was a little short Sergeant and one of my best friends.

We were married Dec. 31,1977 in my parents house. It was a small wedding because we didn't have much money. I had to spend all the money on our plane tickets to get back to Hawaii. A week later we were on our way and our flight took us to LA. And we had to catch a cab to Camp Pendleton to wait for our next flight. The cab driver took the long way around and we ended up paying over a $100.00 dollars for cab fare. I knew we were getting ripped off, but what could I do? I had a new bride and we had our luggage. We couldn't walk to the base because it was already past midnight when our flight arrived in LA.

We finally got to Camp Pendleton California and got checked into this base house. It was one of the scariest nights of our marriage, because there were these giant mosquitoes and big cockroaches flying around the room. I had to be brave for my wife, but I was scared too.

Once we got to Hawaii, things were better. Sergeant Gill was at the airport waiting for us, and took us to his house. It was still kind of strange though because we were living with someone else. Sergeant Gill had a very fast red Road Runner. He loved to talk on the CB radio. His handle was " Chester The Molester" but he was cool.

The Cisco Kid

Base housing was not set up for a Private First Class Marine at that time, so we had to stay with them for a while. Everyone pitched in and helped us get settled in.

I couldn't believe it, the year was 1978 and I was married! I was still trying to figure out who I was and neither one of us knew anything about being married.

Why did I have to be stationed in Hawaii? There were so many beautiful women and my eyes could not stop wandering. I was in paradise, and there were women from every culture. Sometimes when I was walking on Waikiki Beach, I didn't know which direction to look in. I had never seen women like these before except on T.V.

Even though I loved my wife and was very happy, I still felt like something was missing from my life. I was like a child in Disney World with so many things to see. Finally I settled down for a while and our first son Lakinte Monguell Hash was born on April 28, 1978.

Lakinte was our first son and we were so proud of him. Everywhere we went in Hawaii we received so many compliments about what a beautiful, well-behaved child we had.

But once again my mind began to wander. It was like a generational curse. I found myself trying to contact some of my old girlfriends again, Priscilla and Janie Ingram. I managed to locate them and had written letters to them, but one of them was returned undeliverable.

Earnest Grant Hash - United States Marines

Chapter

12

The Big Surprise

When I came home, I was in for a shock. My wife had already opened the mail and had read what I had written. I tried my best to explain it to her, but I was unsuccessful. Before I knew it she had already contacted her mother and she was on her way to Hawaii.

She came, sat down with us, and helped us work things out. I apologized, and we got things back on track. We finally found a church in Hawaii, called Peaceful Holiness Church. It was a wonderful church and the people were so nice to us. They really made us feel welcome. We attended the church faithfully. Here are some of the nice people we met there: Deacon Timothy Smalls and his wife Carol who was from Savannah Georgia, Minister Dawkins from Shreveport La., Bro. and Sis. White, Sis. Hendricks, Bro. Gooch, and Alexander.

Seems like people were just drawn to us, and wanted to help us. SSG. Jessie Smith was a good friend and Sgt. Medina would let me drive his car. It was like everyone had a giving spirit, but I know it was the favor of God as he was looking out for us.

The church would have dinner prepared every Sunday for any one who wanted to eat. I tasted my first piece of "Sock It To Me" cake there and it was very delicious. Sis. Silvia Bell had made it. She later married one of my good friends Lance Corporal Levite. He was a very nice young man, tall and handsome. He was also a baker in The Marine Corps and he could make the best cakes. He knew how to decorate cakes because he had been to baking school in The Marine Corps. We use to make cakes for The Marine Corps Ball and other events. I learned a lot from him.

We stayed with Sgt. Gill until I was able to find my own place out in Kailua, Hawaii. It was a studio where everything was in one room, but it was a perfect fit our family.

We were new over there so we had no credit established and we needed furniture. So we asked my wife's father to co-sign a loan for us. He was a little skeptical but he came through for us.

The apartment we lived in was very small and because of all the water over there we had to deal with a lot of different bugs, big toad frogs, and lizards everyday. The lizards would come under our door and come through the window when we'd be in the shower.

It was crazy, but we survived it all. I didn't have a car so I had to ride my 3-speed bike, which I called a bus to the base everyday. I was a cook in The Marines and some days I would have to be to work at three and four o'clock in the morning. I would have to get up in time to ride my bike to the base, which was about a good five miles from town.

It was very scary, because I didn't know much about Hawaii. It rained a lot and people would offer me rides. Sometimes I had no choice but to get in their cars or be late for duty. God really looked out for me.

Hitchhiking to work was no fun. And then there was the thought that while I was at the base all day, my wife was at home all alone with nothing to do. She could not wander around out in town because it was too dangerous.

There were these big Samoan guys that didn't like Marines and they would always follow us around. But after a while I made a lot of friends by talking on the CB radio. Another world opened up to me then.

The Hawaiian people were very nice to us and time went by pretty fast over there. Soon we were about to have our second child and I had orders to go away on a Float with The Marine Corps.

My Staff Sergeant Gains told me that I would not be able to transfer to another unit in time. He said I would have to go on the float with my unit for six months. But I couldn't leave my wife all alone in a place that she was not familiar with to have a child without me.

I began to pray and talk to God about it. I was determined that I would not leave my wife. I put in my transfer papers and left the rest in God's hands. My Staff Sergeant began to laugh at me because he didn't believe that I would be able to get the transfer through in time.

I was one of his best cooks and he wanted me to go on ship with the unit. But he didn't know whom I knew. Finally time was running out and my transfer papers had not gone through. He began to laugh at me again and make fun of my God. There was only a week left and the orders had not come down from headquarters.

Everyone else had already packed and was ready to go. On the day before the ship was to pull out, the call came. My Commanding Officer said my transfer papers had come through and that I didn't have too go. I was so happy and praising God. Staff Sgt. Gaines was mad at me.

I told him that God would come through for me. And God did. Hallelujah. A few weeks later my daughter was born on Jan. 15, 1980. We named her Necomi Shantel Hash. She was an angel. Soon it would be time to return to Virginia because my time was almost up.

So we moved out of our Apt. and in with some friends from church. Deacon Smalls and his wife opened their doors to us and welcomed us. It was a blessing. My tour of duty was ending in April 1980 and we would be going home.

Before we left to come back to Va. the Pastor ordained me as a Deacon of the church. I preached my first message there.

Chapter

13

Tragedy At Home

While we were away, the house at 401 Hanover caught on fire and my Mom and Dad had to move to another place on Miller Street. This was the second time the house on Hanover had been damaged. Hurricane Hugo had came through and damaged it also.

This house had been through a lot, and we had so many memories, too many to just let it go to somebody else. This was The Hash House. Where would people go if we left the community? But finally there was no other choice. The time had come to let it go.

After Miller Street flooded, and a Herpes outbreak started, everyone had to move off that street. Mom and Dad got a place in Wilmont Farms. But eventually they ended up back on Hanover again.

A lot of people had already moved off the street and things would never be the same again. Some of the old neighbors were still there, like The Barnes

Family and The Browns. Seems like they were there to stay.

So finally we were on our way back home. And it was sure good to go back home once more. We stayed with my parents in The Honey Comb Hide Out again. There was always plenty of room in my parent's house on Hanover Ave.

We had a good marriage and two beautiful children, and it seemed like we were the perfect family. We enjoyed staying there for a while, but knew we needed our own place. We had a family and trying to stay in one room was not working. We needed a separate room for our children.

So I began to look for work and also for an apartment for my family. I went out on Williamson Rd. and they were building a new Arby's, so I placed an application. Before long I was working at Arby's Roast Beef. My dad suggested that I join the Army Reserve to bring in some extra income.

I had been in The Marine Corps and now I wanted to transfer over to The Army Reserve. I had to go through some changes, but I was willing to make the change for my family. By this time my hair had grown back a lot, and I really didn't want to get it cut again. So I tried to get by without cutting it, and just slicking it down, but Major Freeze who was The Commanding Officer at that time would have none of that. So I eventually went and got it cut again.

Being in The Army Reserve was totally different than being in The Marine corps. I had to loose my rank as Lance Corporal and go back to being a Private again. That hurt, but I was even willing to go through all the disrespect of being a Private again for my family.

Then all hell broke loose and I wished we had stayed in Hawaii. The old saying, "All Good Things Must Come To An End" became reality for me. I found out that I had another son, whose name was Arvay L. Robbinson. He was by the same young lady that I had asked before I got married if the child was mine. Remember, she told me no then, that the baby was by another man whom she was going to marry.

But there was no way I could deny him, because he looked just like me. So this caused problems with my wife. During this time a new Apartment complex was being built and we applied for an apartment. (Westwood Village). And low and behold, right across the street lived my son and his family.

Here I was going through hell again. Every time I went to look out the window, I was accused of looking for her or my son. Every time I went outside I could not look that direction, or an argument would start. So my son basically grew up not being able to spend time with me.

This haunted me for along time, because I couldn't go to church or anywhere that they would be. Even now, to this day, this has hurt our Father/Son relationship. I wanted to take care of my responsibility, but my wife made it difficult.

Eventually it got the best of us and we ended up separating. But before we separated we had our third child, Valentino L. Hash. Valentino was born with a heart murmur and breathing problems. He only lived for six (6) months. He was at MCV Hospital in Richmond Va. when he passed away.

I got the call when I was at work at Fred Whitaker Company. He had developed pneumonia and could not be revived. That was the hardest and longest drive I ever had to make.

The day he died was the darkest day of my life. Things never were the same between my wife and I after Valentino died in 1983. Seven (7) years of marriage was gone. I lost my children, Lakinte and

Ne'comi, and even though I tried to see them when I could, things were no longer the same anymore.

Nothing I did was right, and I was alone. But suddenly girls began to show up that said they had been in love with me all their lives. This was news to me. But that was not what I wanted now. I tried to find Priscilla again, but was unsuccessful. I tried dating again, but nothing could fill the void in my life.

I would sit in church and cry because I had lost my family. I tried to get them back, but it was not to be. I had to except the fact that I had to start all over again. I began to see a few young ladies, from time to time, but it was not the same.

Chapter

14

A New Beginning

It was 1986 and we had moved back into our house once more at 401 Hanover Ave. The Honey Comb Hideout had been fixed up again after it had burnt up. We were home again. I was working two jobs trying to fill the void, plus I was in The Army Reserve.

One day these girls moved in across the street from us, and before we knew it we found ourselves watching them. We wanted to know who they were but we were trying to be discreet. We would sit upstairs in the window and watch them across the street. They tried not to let us see them looking at us, but they were looking at my brothers and me. We would see them come out the house each morning to go to school, because they had to walk all the way across the dump to get to the bus stop.

So we would watch them go to school and then come home in the evening. They were fast walkers and kind of stuck up at first. But my brothers and I wore them down. Eventually they began to talk to us.

The older girl caught my eye. Her name was Chantel, but she had her sights on someone else. So the other sister and I started talking. We were just friends at first, but we became closer because we would talk everyday when she came home from school.

We began to like each other and wanted to see each other everyday, and spend more time with each other. Her name was Shanta A. Burwell. She began to tell me her plans of what she wanted in life. The thing is, she was only 17 years old and I was 30 at the time.

She was very mature and knew what she wanted out of life. But I felt like I was robbing the cradle. Still, we continued to talk each day and got to know each other better. One day I had to drive all of them to New Jersey to see their family. There were four of them that moved here to Virginia. I had never been to New Jersey, let alone driven that far by myself. But trying to be the man, I took on the task. The trip started out fine, except my radiator started to over heat.

But eventually as the sun went down the car began to drive better. It was an old, green, 1973 Chevy Impala. It had no air condition or front or rear defrost. Suddenly it began to rain, at first lightly and then very hard. My heart began to beat faster. Most of the girls had fallen asleep and I was all alone trying to figure out where to go.

The rain began to fog up my windows and I couldn't see where I was going. I wanted to pull over but thought I should try and keep moving. Things got worse and I was trying to take a rag and clean my window so I could see and I began to swerve across the road. And then it happened, red lights began to flash and the siren came on.

I looked for a place to pull over and then the police came up to the car. He asked for my license and registration. He asked did I know why he pulled me over, I said, no sir. He said I was all over the road. I began to explain to him what was happening and that we were on our way to Newark, New Jersey, and my defroster was not working.

So he shined his flashlight all through the car and saw that I was with four young ladies, and as he checked my license, he saw that I had no record, so he gave me a warning and told me to be careful. I said, thank you sir, and began to start the car again. As I pulled off, I thanked God that I did not get a ticket and that we were safe.

Still, I had no ideal where we were and I forgot to ask the officer for directions. So we began to go on and on. Finally we came to a service station and I pulled in for directions.

To my surprise, we were almost in Connecticut. We had to turn around and go back and get on the right highway. Here I was with a car full of girls whose lives were in my hand, and only God knew where we were headed. I had never been so scared in all my life. But finally we made it to New Jersey. We pulled up at Momma Sarah's house.

I was so tired, sleepy, and nervous, because I was meeting Shanta's Grand Mother and family for the first time. This was a trying time for me. I felt so alone. They were home but I was in a strange land, around strange people. Shanta was so busy with all her friends at The Lincoln Hotel that I felt she forgot that I was even there.

So I got a little angry and did something stupid. I wandered off by myself, once again thinking I was the big man. But I was in unfamiliar territory, and didn't know where I was going. I walked around for about an hour and finally made my way back to the hotel. Shanta later told me that I was in East Orange, and that I could have gotten killed.

My car broke down while I was there and somebody stole my hubcaps off my car. So Shanta's father helped me find another carburetor for my car. I was ready to go home. All of her family was very nice and made me feel welcome, but there is no place like home, and I was ready to go. I met some interesting people while I was there though.

I met Bob, whom she said took care of them and was like family to them, also her other sister Yvonne, and her boy friend Joseph. He was nice. They helped us get on the right road to get back home, after they took us shopping. Home never looked so good. My car did good and got us back home.

We all were a lot closer after that trip. And I got to know them really good. They were a good family. Eventually we decided that we wanted to get married. So one day when we were at Chic- Fillet, I popped the question. I got down on my knees and asked her to marry me. I figured nothing in this world is guaranteed, so why not take a chance. So I did. She said yes, and we made plans and set the date.

I didn't know that her sisters were going to be so upset, but they were. They did not want us to get married. But we were determined and we set a date and stuck to it. We didn't have a big wedding, but we got married at her Grand Mother Irma Harper's house. My Uncle Clyde married us. He liked Shanta. He called her country.

We didn't have a place of our own yet so we stayed with my mother and father across the street. There was always room at The Honey Comb Hideout. We had a wonderful time there. Shanta was still in school so I would take her to school and pick her up in the evenings.

We had a room upstairs and it was really nice. But we knew we needed our own place soon. One year later our first child was born. She was so beautiful, and we named her Cyndle Alora Duneay Hash. Cyndle, because she was our Cinderella. We were watching this movie called The Ewoks, and the little girl in the movie was named Cyndle. Alora Duneay came from the movie named "Willow". The little baby was named Alora Dunin. And of course Hash came from us.

She was a special child from the very beginning. Everyone loved her and we knew she would be someone great. Cyndle loved church and she was so cool. We use to go to pick up her mother from Dominion Business College, and we would be in the car listening to music. She loved all my music. She would learn all the words real fast.

Chapter

15

Our First Apartment

Once again the house on Hanover caught on fire and we were forced to move. We found a place in Landsdown Apartments. We finally had our own place. We had some nice neighbors, who became our friends. Across the street was a very nice older gentleman who had a lot of rose bushes in his yard. He would bring my wife different color roses from time to time.

Cyndle was around two or three now and she was beginning to learn her A B C's and numbers. We bought her some blocks and different puzzles to help her. Cyndle was a fast learner but had some difficulty in remembering from time to time. But she was our first little girl and we were determined to teach her.

Eventually she began to catch on. Cyndle's room was upstairs and sometimes she would wander off into our bedroom. So one day we were looking for her and found her in our room. Cyndle had gotten hold to a pair of scissors and had cut chunks out of her hair.

She had beautiful hair and now it was messed up. We were very upset at her, but what could we do? She was only a curious child.

Cyndle also had another mishap; she got into the Vicks Vapor Rub and put it all over her face. All of a sudden we heard her screaming upstairs and we came a running. Cyndle's face was red all over and her nose was running down to her chin. She was screaming real loud. We rushed her to the emergency room.

Our Aunt Judy who is a nurse at Community hospital helped us. They had to get all the Vapor Rub off her, dilate her eyes, and put her under a black fluorescent light to see if any more was on her. It was so funny but scary to see her crying and screaming with her face on fire like that.

Because Cyndle was so beautiful and smart we knew that she was going to be someone special. But as time came for her to start school, her mother couldn't bare seeing her off. As she took her to the bus tears began to flow. Our first child was off on a big adventure. She was leaving home for the first time without us.

By this time we had moved back in with my parents at 2506 Portland Ave. Our rent had gotten outrageous and we could not afford it anymore. Shanta was in College and my income was not enough to keep things going. So my parents graciously accepted us back into their home.

Also my daughter Necomi, from a previous marriage came to live with us. She was facing some difficulties of her own, and needed a change. So now Cyndle had a big sister to play with her and teach her different things. Of course I was still in The Army Reserve and had to go away from time to time. This was hard on everyone because sometimes I would be gone for weeks.

During Desert Storm I had to go away for three months to run a Dinning Facility for the Army Reserve at Fort Bragg N. C. This was back in 1990. This was a new experience for me, having to feed so many soldiers and stay within the budget. But I knew that God was with me and that I could do it.

During this time we were having some problems in our marriage, so my wife decided to go on an adventure, to go see her sister Chantel. She hit the highway with a car full of children all by herself. She had great determination because they made it. I really missed them and it turned out that she missed me too. We worked things out and I came home on a few days leave.

We loaded up the car and they went to stay with me for a few days at Fort Bragg. While we were there someone broke into our car and stole my stereo system and my speakers from my car. I had spent a lot of money on that equipment and that really hurt. I filed a police report and eventually they reimbursed me for everything.

But low and behold my transmission went out on me and I had to end up spending a large portion of my check to get my car fixed so we could get back home.

Life in the Army Reserve was good and I made a lot of friends, SSgt Charles Smith was my right hand man. I learned a lot from him. He was my Sgt. along with SSgt. Alfred Andrews. My dad was also apart of this unit when I first transferred over to The Army Reserve.

I learned all I could from these guys and eventually SFC Roy Kendrick took over as Dining Facility Manager. We got along great. But SFC Kendrick was very ambitious and went to Warrant Officer School. Before long he became a Warrant Officer. We had a lot of cooks and they all were very good. There was SSG. James Perdue, Sgt. James Lemons, Sgt Wiley P.J. Brooks, SSG. Charles Smith and from time to time different cooks would come through.

I remember Michael Davis, Leon Grant, Spec. Napier, and too many others to name. We became good friends with a lot of other cooks from other units as well: SFC Woodley, SFC Nathaniel Williams who I called Fearless Fly, Sgt. Charles Poindexter, SSgt. Phillip Bolden (deceased), and Sgt. Nelson Milner. I can't remember all their names, but I can see them in my mind.

The cook section was very special. We would get up early in the morning to prepare meals and we overcame some very difficult times together. We were family. Each one of them was like my very own brother or sister. I still have a lot of pictures of all the guys. I look at them from time to time and the memories make me miss them all so much.

During my time in The Army Reserve I received several medals. I received The Army Commendation Medal in 1990, The Army Achievement Medal in 1991 and again in 1993. Before that I received The Good Conduct Medal from The Marine Corps in 1980 along with a Note worthy Achievement in 1978. I was highly respected by all my peers as well as all my superiors.

They believed in me and this gave me confidence and the courage to believe I could accomplish anything. Everything that I put my hands to would prosper. I was promoted to SFC in Nov. 0f 92. The 90's were a difficult time for the military. They began to down size and do away with certain units and mine was one of them. They decided that the cooks were no longer needed.

Also during this time my second daughter was born on Dec. 28, 1993. We named her Fabrae' Jonteal Hash. She had a set of lungs on her. Shanta was working at night and I was working during the day. So when Shanta would leave to go to work at night, she would start screaming because Shanta had spoiled her during the day.

My task was to get some sleep at night so I could get up for work the next day. Fabrae' was determined that that was not going to happen. After awhile she began to get use to me and we both began to get some sleep.

But something else happened that year. We were staying down in the basement and had to go upstairs in order to get to the restroom. After Shanta had Fabrae' this was difficult for her to do. We tried to make things easy for her so she wouldn't have to climb the stairs, but Shanta didn't like that. One day she was up making the bed. All of a sudden she screamed and started twirling around in the floor. She was having a seizure. I had never seen anything like this before, and it really scared me.

Cyndle was screaming and I told her to go upstairs and call 911. The ambulance came and took her to the hospital. This was the beginning of a turbulent time for us. They did X-rays and said that everything was all right. Shanta did good for a while and the seizures went away. We thought that maybe this was a one-time thing. Our family was getting bigger and we needed another place to stay. My Aunt Edna and Uncle Clyde had acquired a place and they rented it to us.

By this time it was 1995 and Joshua was born. Joshua would complete our family because the doctor said that Shanta could not have any more children or it could be dangerous to her health. My oldest son Arvay wanted to come and live with us at this time. So now we were a family of 7: Arvay, Necomi, Cyndle, Fabrae' and Joshua, along with Shanta and myself.

But it so happened that the house that Uncle Clyde and Aunt Edna were living in was being sold and they needed a place to move to. We were living in their house so we had to find another place. The search was on. We looked at several places and finally found an apartment on 10th St. in South West.

I was still in the Army Reserve and it had come time for the cooks to disband. The final word had come down from headquarters. They gave us different options in order to try to keep us in the unit, but I knew things would never be the same.

Different branches of the service would come to the Reserve Center to talk to us and try to get us to join their unit. I had put my life into the 80th Division and I just couldn't bring myself to go anywhere else. They asked me to be an Instructor in my unit but I was a cook and couldn't see myself doing anything else. So I decided to take the early retirement that was offered me.

The time had come to move on to something else. I had been a singer all my life but had never written any songs or tried to sing on my own. But all of a sudden all these songs began to fill my mind. I decided to find a recording studio and someone to put some music to my songs. I was told about Off The Hook Studio.

So I went to check them out and sat down with Jermaine English, and he began to work with me. This guy was awesome on the keyboards and really knew what he was doing. I found out that I had a lot of work to do in order to get ready to record a CD. I had to work on my breathing technique and pronouncing my words correctly.

Jermaine was easy to work with and he respected me as a singer. He knew that I sang in a group years ago, but I was a backup singer. I led a few songs but I was no leader. Finally I was ready to record. It was a long process and Jermaine played some of the most beautiful music I had ever heard. It was like he knew what I was looking for.

I had written five songs. The title cut was "Jesus Is Mine" along with "Lord I Love You (Yes I Do)", "Seedtime and Harvest", "I'll Go All The Way", and "Jesus Loves Me". My CD was finished and I was so happy. I had a feeling of accomplishment. At last my dreams were coming true, I was a songwriter and a Recording Artist. My family was so proud of me, but I was faced with a problem. I had no distributor and no money to get one. A CD cannot sell if it cannot get to the right people. Also I had to find someone to reproduce copies of my CD. WTOY a radio station in Roanoke began to play it on the air, but even if people liked it, I still had no way of getting it to them.

Then I teamed up with Elder Larry Manns and he helped me make copies of my CD. It began to sell very well locally. I knew in order to make the big time I would have to get it in someone else's hands. We did a few concerts together and the CD continued to play on the radio.

Everyone that heard it loved it. I found out about a company called CD Baby, which is an Internet CD store for Independent Artist. So I contacted them and sent them some of my CD's. Now my CD is reaching the world. People all over the world can listen to clips of my music and order it if they like it. I know it is just a matter of time before the right people hear it and it goes worldwide.

During a dream one night God showed me singing with my daughters, Cyndle and Fabrae'. The next morning I told them about my dream and they loved the ideal. We began to practice and our voices blended well together. I began to write some new songs.

God was giving me one song after another from His word. At first we began to sing acappella because we had no one to put music to our songs. Jermaine had moved to Richmond Va. God had already given me the melodies in my mind when I was writing the songs. So I knew basically what I wanted.

Elder Larry Manns had asked me to become his partner in the studio and to come up with a name for it. So I prayed and asked God about it. Several names came to mind but one name stuck with me, Favor Of God Studio. I knew we would need the favor of God in order for this to work.

Elder Manns was a good friend at the time and I thought that we would be able to get along well since we use to work together in The National Motor Club together. Things went along well for a while. We even found other groups and singers to join us.

I took some of my songs with me to the studio one day and let him listen to them. He liked them very much and decided that he wanted to be the one to record them and put the music to them. So I told my daughters about it and they were so excited. We decided to do a CD together. We became Minister Bernard Hash & Glory2.

This is the name that God had given me for our company and the name that had been on my license plate for some time now: Glory 2 Productions. I liked the name. We went to Favor of God Studio and began to work on our CD. Larry's wife was very nice to us and she really loved the girls. He also had a group called "The Friends Of God".

Chapter

16

Our First CD

It was an exciting time for us. I would go over to the studio and work with Larry to lay down the lead tracks. I had also written some poetry and decided that I wanted to try something different. So along with the songs I added a few of my poems on the CD. Things were going very well. The drummer was very good and he had a digital set.

I took my daughters to the studio and we listened to the music for the first song. Wow, it sounded so good and we were very impressed with the sound of it. We really thought that Larry was going to do an excellent job for us. But something happened and instead of him taking the proper time for each song, he began to rush and just hurry us through the CD. Larry hated to have to redo anything.

The CD was almost complete. Somewhere along the way Larry and the drummer had a disagreement and the drummer left. So now we were stuck with synthetic drums. Larry did the best he could do but it was not the same. Finally the CD was finished. As we all sat down to listen to it we knew that something was missing.

We wished we had the money to do it over but we had limited funds. Living in Roanoke Va. was hard because there were not many recording studios in the area. But I believe that because we tried, we inspired many others in Roanoke to give recording a try.

October 2003 we decided to work on a Christmas CD. So we each set out to write songs to go on it. There was Elder David Baylor, Elder James Hardy, The Friends Of God, and our group Minister Bernard Hash & Glory 2. In November we came together with what we had and started laying down the tracks.

Each group's style was different and at first it didn't seem like it was going to work. But eventually we had to help each other and try to blend the right voices together for each song. I had written " Its Christmas Time" and "Ring In Our Hearts".

"It's Christmas Time" became the title of the CD. Larry worked really hard and finally the project was finished. He decided that he wanted to do all the mixing and work himself. After he had finished he called each one of us and gave us our copies of the CD. When I got home I put it in the CD player. As we all listened to it, we discovered that Larry had put the same song on the CD twice.

I gave Larry a call and explained to him what had happened, that he had made a mistake. Larry wanted me to accept the CD's as is and sell them, but I told him I could not do that. Then, he wanted me to pay him again to redo the CD's. So I went to the studio and we finally got the CD's corrected.

We had a Christmas concert scheduled so that we could promote the CD. Larry was very angry with me because he had to do the CD's over so he refused to come and sing at the concert. He also would not accept any of my phone calls. It turned out that Elder David Baylor was unable to make it that day also.

Elder Hardy and my group went on with the concert. It was a very beautiful concert and everyone enjoyed it. To this day Elder Manns has not contacted me or even answered any of the letters I sent him. I have tried to apologize to him by calling him as well as writing to him.

I really miss his friendship and wish we could have worked things out. It's sad when two Ministers of the gospel can't get along with each other and work things out. Christ said that we must forgive one another or He would not forgive us.

So I continue to try to communicate with him although I have had no luck to date. When I see him I blow my car horn at him, hopefully to let him know that I still care. Sometimes I wonder, when he's up preaching does he think about this situation? I pray that one day he will be able to forgive. He still uses the name that I gave him for the studio as well as the artwork that I drew on the building. He also kept all my original demos and never returned any of my work to me.

But my daughters and I have moved on. God has opened other doors for us. We all wrote a book of poetry together called "Hope For Despair" poems of life. A print on demand company called Xlibris published it for us and we have been on TV several times singing together. Each year we have been asked to sing at "The National Day Of Prayer" which is celebrated each first Thursday in May.

Ms. Lindsey Wray of Roanoke Times World News has interviewed us. And we have been in the newspaper several times. So the dream that God gave me for our group is happening for us.

Now here we are in the year 2006 and it's graduation time for our daughter Cyndle. She has more than exceeded our expectations for her. Cyndle is graduating with honors. She received an IB Diploma, Key Club, Beta Club, The Governors Seal, and Advanced Studies Seal. We were invited to several banquets in her honor as well.

Also a miracle happened, Cyndle's grandfather from New Jersey came in to see us. We had not seen him for about 8 years. He had not been to Roanoke for thirty-three years. It was so wonderful and we had a great time together. One of our friends from church also came and spent time with us. Her name is Angela Baker. She has become part of our family now.

Uncle Joe, my wife's father John Burwell, as well as Granny Harper came to our house. Shanta's cousins Crystal Burwell and Franswa also came. We all sat down together and had dinner. We had a wonderful time. Everyone really enjoyed themselves.

Finally the big day was here. It was time for Cyndle to walk across the stage and receive her diploma. I had my camera and plenty of film. I tried to get as many pictures as I could, because this would be a memorable day. We were so excited to see our daughter walk across that stage. Cyndle really worked hard and deserved everything she was receiving.

Cyndle also received a full scholarship to James Madison University. She will be attending in the fall of 2006. It will be a happy day as well as a sad day to see our daughter go off on her own for the first time. But we pray and believe that she will do well and be the Lawyer that she wants to be one day. She will be studying Criminal Justice and Psychology.

Our other daughter Fabrae' is following in her footsteps. She has become an IB student as well. She is amazing. I believe she will be a scientist one day and discover some marvelous things.

As for our son Joshua, well that story still remains to be written. I could write another whole book just about him. I believe he will be great and accomplish great things some day.

As my story comes to an end, I hope that you have enjoyed it and that you will come back for part two. So long.

THE END

www.ingramcontent.com/pod-product-compliance
Ingram Content Group UK Ltd.
Pitfield, Milton Keynes, MK11 3LW, UK
UKHW022210230426
12048UKWH00016BA/765